M.P. ROBERTSON studied illustration at Kingston University. He is an internationally acclaimed author and illustrator of children's books. His many books for Frances Lincoln include *The Great Dragon Rescue*, *The Egg*, *Frank 'n' Stan*, *Food Chain*, *Hieronymus Betts and His Unusual Pets* and *Ice Trap!*, written by Meredith Hooper. He lives with his family in Wiltshire. When he isn't writing and illustrating, he enjoys visiting schools to share his love of drawing and stories. To find out more about Mark's books or to book a visit, please go to **www.mprobertson.com**

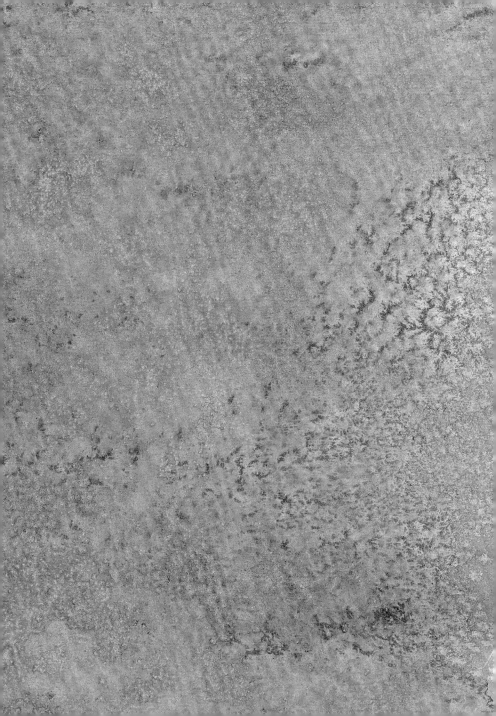

To Bob Gammack for the great times
at South Ash

Text and Illustrations copyright M.P. Robertson 2005, 2014

The right of M.P. Robertson to be identified as the author and illustrator
of this Work has been asserted by him in accordance with the Copyright,
Designs and Patent Act, 1988.

First published in Great Britain in 2005.

This early reader edition first published in Great Britain and in the USA in
2014 by Frances Lincoln Children's Books, 74-77 White Lion Street,
London N1 9PF

www.franceslincoln.com

A CIP catalogue record for this book is available from the British Library.

978-1-84780-550-8

Printed in China

1 3 5 7 9 8 6 4 2

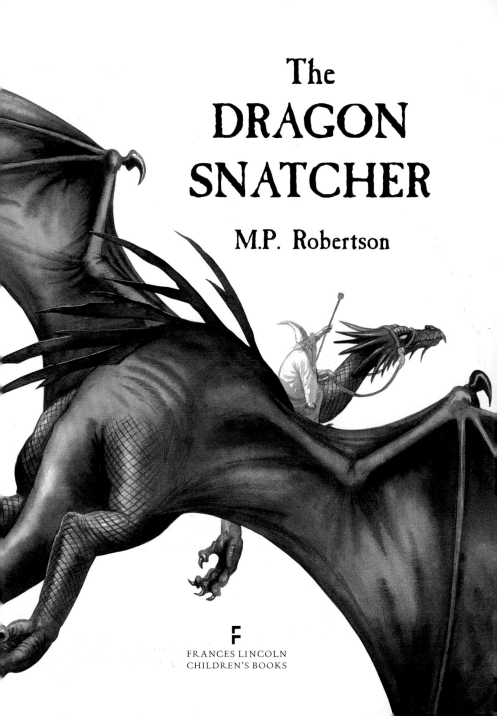

The
DRAGON
SNATCHER

M.P. Robertson

F

FRANCES LINCOLN
CHILDREN'S BOOKS

Snow lay deep on the ground.

George was happy reading his books. It was a
night to be lost in a story.

Suddenly, George heard a noise in the chicken house.

George peered out of his window. Looking up at him was his dragon. He had a worried look in his yellow eye. George threw a blanket around his shoulders and climbed out on to the dragon's neck.

He clung tightly as they were carried on
the North Wind to a land that was neither
Here nor There.

They soared over mountains, until George saw a dark castle that cut through the ice. The dragon landed silently and hid beneath the drawbridge.

George knew it was not only the cold that made his
dragon shiver. There was something evil inside.

George entered the castle alone. He came to a
courtyard where a soot-black dragon stood guard.
George sneaked past, keeping to the shadows.

He found a staircase that wound its way up through the heart of the castle. At the top of the stairs was a heavy wooden door. George pushed it open.

He couldn't believe what he found inside – shelves and shelves of eggs covered in frost. They all had labels like The Rock Gobbler to Horny Cave Dweller.

They were dragon eggs! There was only one empty
space left to fill. Its label read: The Lesser-Spotted
Red Crest – extremely rare.

**The Lesser-Spotted
Red Crest**

extremely rare

Suddenly George was startled by a noise on the
stairs. Quickly he hid behind a large egg.

A crooked old wizard with a beard of frost entered the room. George felt a shiver as the room became icy cold. The wizard cackled, "Only one more to find. Then I will free the land of these creatures."
He stared into an globe of ice, and began to mumble strange spells. In the centre of the globe, George could see the mountains around the castle.

The wizard searched the mountains, looking everywhere. On top of the highest peak was a twisted tree. There was a dragon's nest among its branches, and in the nest was a glowing, orange egg.
"There you are, my little one," hissed the wizard. "Soon my collection will be complete!"

The wizard ran down the stairs into the courtyard and mounted the black dragon. George leaned out of the window and whistled for his dragon.

George leapt on to his dragon's back as it flew
in front of the window.

They followed the black dragon at a distance.
Soon George spotted the twisted tree and – oh no!
The wizard was crawling on to a branch towards the
dragon egg.

But George had a plan. He used his blanket as a net to snatch the egg from the wizard.

Then the chase began! A ball of fire came whistling past George's ear and crashed into the mountain. The black dragon was belching fire at them.

George's dragon flitted about trying to avoid the fireballs. It was difficult to see through the smoke. He turned too quickly and crashed into the face of a mountain.

George had a soft landing in the snow, but the egg fell from the blanket and he watched as it rolled down the mountain and landed at the wizard's feet.

The wizard said, "It's mine!," holding up the egg.

But the egg began to glow as if there was a fire inside.

It burned hotter and hotter until it was too hot for the wizard to hold. The egg was hatching!
The wizard looked shocked as a tiny red dragon came out of the egg. Then he sank to his knees, picking up pieces of shell.
"The last egg," he sobbed. "It's broken!"

But the baby dragon was looking at the wizard with
love in his eyes.

"He thinks you are his mother," said George.

"I am not your mother!" said the wizard.

He stared fiercely into the bright yellow eyes of the
dragon. The dragon stared back lovingly.

The wizard's heart began to melt.
Back at the castle a wonderful thing happened . . .
The wizard's icy spell had been broken!

The wizard led the dragon towards the castle.
"He will make a good mother," thought George.
And as he flew over the castle, a rainbow of
dragons filled the sky.

George headed for home, happy that once again dragons would fly free in the land that is neither Here nor There.

Collect the TIME TO READ books:

978-1-84780-476-1

978-1-84780-475-4

978-1-84780-477-8

978-1-84780-478-5

978-1-84780-543-0

978-1-84780-544-7

978-1-84780-542-3

978-1-84780-545-4

978-1-84780-549-2

978-1-84780-551-5

978-1-84780-552-2

978-1-84780-550-8

Frances Lincoln titles are available from all good bookshops.
You can also buy books and find out more about your favourite titles,
authors and illustrators on our website: www.franceslincoln.com